P9-AOX-007

The Mixed-Up Mask Mystery

A Fletcher Mystery

The Mixed-Up Mask Mystery

by **Elizabeth Levy**

Illustrated by **Mordicai Gerstein**

Aladdin Paperbacks

New York London Toronto Sydney Singapore

To Tony

If you purchased this book without a cover, you should be aware that this book is stolen property. It was reported as "unsold and destroyed" to the publisher, and neither the author nor the publisher has received any payment for this "stripped book."

This book is a work of fiction. Any references to historical events, real people, or real locales are used fictitiously. Other names, characters, places, and incidents are the product of the author's imagination, and any resemblance to actual events or locales or persons, living or dead, is entirely coincidental.

First Aladdin Paperbacks edition January 2003
Text copyright © 2003 by Elizabeth Levy
Illustrations copyright © 2003 by Mordicai Gerstein

ALADDIN PAPERBACKS
An imprint of Simon & Schuster Children's Publishing Division
1230 Avenue of the Americas, New York, NY 10020

All rights reserved, including the right of
reproduction in whole or in part in any form.

Also available in an Aladdin library edition.
Designed by Lisa Vega
The text of this book was set in ACaslon Regular.

Printed in the United States of America
2 4 6 8 10 9 7 5 3 1

Library of Congress Control Number for the library edition is 2002110446
ISBN 0-689-84628-2

Contents

One

Fat Basset Hound Dancing!   1

Two

A Mask of a French Fry   6

Three

Put a Sock in It   19

Four

Chew on That, You Rodent!   31

Five

Liar! Liar!
Pants Really Are on Fire!   46

Six

Who Would Ruin the Dance?   57

Seven

Trip the Light Fantastic   69

One

Fat Basset Hound Dancing!

"Fletcher! Wake up! Wake up!" There is nothing worse than having a flea yelling in your ear on a warm summer day.

I shook my ears. "What's wrong?"

"Summer!" said Jasper, the flea who lives on me. "All you do is sleep."

"What's not to like about summer? The kids home from school, barbecues in the backyard, plastic pools to wade in."

"I'm bored," complained Jasper. "I'm so bored, I could bite you on the butt. I'm going to do six

CLOSE-UP OF JASPER
DOING SIX SOMERSAULTS
ON FLETCHER'S NOSE

somersaults on your nose. Watch me!"

"A somersaulting flea is quite spectacular," I told Jasper. "But so is snoozing in the shade."

"Let's not snooze away this fine day! There must be a park we can romp in."

"Romping is overrated," I muttered. "Basset hounds don't romp." I waddled over to the wading pool where Jill and her best friend, Gwen, were dangling their feet. This was our first summer together. Jill patted me behind my ears and dripped a little water on my nose. Bliss!

"I'm bored. I wish we had something to do," said Gwen.

"Gwen thinks summer is boring too!" squeaked

Jasper. He and Gwen are a lot alike. Neither knows how to appreciate a good nap.

Just then, Jill's mother came out to the backyard. "Hi, kids," she said. "I just got a flyer about the new park." She handed the flyer to Jill, who read it out loud. "Midsummer madness fling! A masked ball to celebrate the opening of our new park! Come to the Arts and Crafts Center and make your own mask! Music and food! Hot dogs for everyone!"

I wagged my tail at the word *hot dog*. Many dogs hate the word *hot dog*, but not me. I'm proud to be named after any encased meats. They're my favorites.

FLETCHER AS A HOT DOG

"Look, said Gwen, noticing my tail, "Fletcher wants to come to the ball."

Jill got up and held out her hands. "Fletcher, do you want to dance?" she asked me.

I rolled my eyes. "Dance with her!" demanded Jasper.

"I look silly dancing!" I muttered. Humans and fleas love to see dogs dance, but I hate to prance on just my back feet. It makes me feel like I'm going to topple over.

"Do the jitterbug, do the jitterbug!" Jasper kept shouting in my ear.

"I won't dance. Don't ask me!" I said to Jasper.

"He doesn't seem to want to dance," said Jill.

"You fool!" shrieked Jasper. "Jill took us in and gave us a home, and you won't even dance with her."

"Look," I said, "I hate to disappoint her. But really—a fat basset hound dancing in the summer heat, it just isn't me." I circled Gwen and Jill three times and lay down. I wished everyone would stop talking about dancing.

Two

A Mask of a French Fry

In the afternoon, we all went to the new park so Gwen and Jill could find out about making their masks. Jasper was thrilled to be on the move.

"How do you think I would look in an elephant mask?" he asked. "I've always thought I'd look good in a trunk."

"I agree. You'd look good in a trunk that was being shipped to Singapore. You're quite the annoying flea. You're always waking me up."

JASPER IN AN ELEPHANT MASK

"They should make you a mask of a sloth. You know, those creatures that hang from trees and sleep all day."

"I thought those were bats," I said.

Suddenly the path turned dark, and I wondered if there were any bats listening to us. The trees were so tall almost no sunlight came through.

"When I was your age," said Jill's mother, "we thought Old Man McKrieger's house was haunted. The old man never mowed his lawn. He let the land next to him grow into this big forest. It was weird to have a forest in the middle of the suburbs. We used to say he was a warlock."

"What's a warlock?" Jill asked just at the same time that Jasper whispered the same question into my ear.

"It's a male witch," said Jill's mother. "He wasn't one at all. He never had any children, or even pets.

FEMALE WITCH   MALE WITCH   SAND-WICH

When he died, he gave the land and his house to the town for a park. Some cousin thought he should leave his property to him or her, but it got settled. Now the town is having a party."

The house in the middle of the woods looked more than a little spooky. There was a huge iron spiked fence around it. I heard a gnawing noise coming from a branch above the fence.

I looked up to see a squirrel balanced on its long furry tail. It saw me, yelled "Dog!," and darted farther up on the tree.

"I'm not the squirrel-chasing kind of dog," I told him.

"All dogs are our enemies," said the squirrel.

"Not me," I tried to explain. "Seriously, what would I do with a squirrel if I ever caught it?"

The squirrel took a nut and tossed it down at me. It landed on my head.

Jasper narrowly jumped out of its way. His antennae were shaking in anger. "Watch where you drop your nuts!" he yelled up to the squirrel.

The squirrel just laughed.

"Hey, you!" I growled. "You almost hit my friend."

"A dog with a flea for a friend is a poor excuse for a hound," said the squirrel.

He threw another nut down at me. This time he hit Jill on the head. "Ouch!" she shouted.

"Now, look here!" I growled. "It's one thing to aim at me, but don't aim at my owner. She's an innocent girl. Stop with the nut-throwing. You could hurt someone."

"Owner," sniffed the squirrel. "Nobody owns Puck!"

Puck darted farther up the tree.

A park ranger came out and sat down on a rocker on the front porch of the house. She was eating a sandwich. A man was pacing up and down in front of her. I thought I got a whiff of salami. I managed to get myself to the ranger's side in case she felt like sharing.

"You sure *can* move fast when you want to," whispered Jasper.

"We're here to find out about making masks for the ball," said Jill.

The ranger looked at me. "Your pooch has got quite a long schnozzle on him already. Were you going to make him a mask, too?"

Just then the man's head whipped around. "Brilliant, Miss Macintosh," he said. "Dancing dogs at the ball."

"Oh goody!" said Jasper, clapping his antennae together. "We'll go to the ball."

"Fletcher would be great in a mask," said Jill. "He could be an elephant or a monkey. He'd look funny in elephant ears."

I am proud of my ears. Unlike my stubby tail, my ears are exactly what a basset hound's ears

ROME
JASPER
ITALY ON FLETCHER'S EAR

should be. Long and silky, and I have Italy on the right one.

"Mr. Fernbach," said Miss Macintosh. "I was only kidding about this kid making a mask for her

dog. Dogs at the dance could get very messy. People would have to watch where they put their feet."

I was a little insulted. Jill cleans up after me every time I poop, and I try very hard never to go on walkways. I prefer to do my business behind a tree.

"I'm Fiedler Fernbach," said the man, extending his hand to Jill's mother. "I'm in charge of public relations for the park. A masked ball for pets! We could get national coverage for this."

"Fletcher's got the map of the world on him," said Jill. "Maybe you could get worldwide coverage."

"Who is Fletcher?" asked Fiedler Fernbach.

"Stand up! Stand up!" Jasper shouted at me. "We could get on TV!"

"Him!" said Jill, pointing down to me. "See, he's got all the continents on him. I could make him a mask that looks like a moon. Then he could be the earth and the moon all at once."

"Isn't that romantic?" said Jasper.

"I'm not sure I want to be the moon," I said. "I'd rather be the sun. The sun gets to sit still. The moon

CLOSE-UP OF JASPER

FIEDLER FERNBACH

gallops around the earth every twenty-four hours."

"Actually, your belly's so big it could block out the sun," squawked a voice high above me. It was the darned Puck.

Just then I heard a cell phone go off. Miss Macintosh flicked open her phone. She made a face when she looked at who was calling, but she turned it on. "Aunt Julie, I'm working right now. Yes, I ate the sandwich, thank you." As Miss Macintosh was talking, she packed up her lunch. I definitely got the sweet-sharp scent of salami. Whoever Aunt Julie was, she had good taste.

Mr. Fernbach was looking at Miss Macintosh. He rubbed his hands together. "This is no time to be making personal calls," he said. "We've got to notify the local radio and TV stations."

He looked down at Gwen and Jill. "You have a job to do, kids. Spread the word to all your friends to bring their pets tomorrow to make papier-mâché masks."

"What's papier-mâché?" Jasper asked.

"I don't know," I admitted. "But it sounds French, and I like things that sound French. Think French fries."

"You're going to get a French fry mask?" asked Jasper.

"Sure," I said. "Why not? I wonder if Jill can make it with ketchup."

FLETCHER IN A FRENCH FRY MASK

Three
Put a Sock in It

Gwen and Jill told everyone they knew that the party was going to include pets. The next day when we went to the park, I was happy to see Isabella and her dog, Felicity, a very dainty dachshund. Roger, a bulldog, was there with his owner, Noah. Sam had brought his pet snake, Isaac. There were a number of kids with dogs I had never seen before. Ellen brought Spencer, a little Chihuahua, and Liz was there with Buddy, a brown-and-white Lhasa apso who thought he was a lot tougher than he looked. Sarah-Kate and David were there with Bernie. He told us he was a mutt and he was proud of it. He was huge. Somewhere in him, there was a lot of greyhound.

We all started sniffing each other. I sniffed Roger's rear end. Bernie leaned down and sniffed my rear.

"Ohhh, that tickles!" exclaimed Jasper.

"Do you know you have a flea on you?" asked Bernie.

"I do," I said. "Jasper's my buddy!"

"A flea can't be a buddy," said Buddy, getting his nose under my leg. "I'm Buddy." When humans meet, they shake hands or give each other a hug, but you can really tell a lot from a good sniff.

"I don't have any fleas," said Felicity, putting her nose right up to mine.

I sniffed her. She did smell rather sweet. "Did you just have a bath?" I asked her.

"Dachshunds are naturally free of doggy odors," said Felicity.

"And rather full of herself, too," whispered Jasper into my ear.

I heard high-pitched squeaking coming from above us. I looked above to see Puck, the same mean, bushy-tailed squirrel we had met the day before. He was joined by a couple of other squirrels. Tree squirrels are usually a pretty solitary bunch, but this group seemed to be banded together.

"Puck, you're right! There are more of them here today," said one of them.

"I told you," said Puck. He was clearly their leader. "You let one of them in, and they come in packs. First it was that fat, blobby-looking one, and now he's brought his friends. Look at that tiny one that looks like a hot dog without a bun. Is she ugly or what?"

"Hey!" I growled. "Don't call me a blob! It happens that basset hounds are born low to the ground. And Felicity is far from ugly."

"Thank you, Fletcher," said Felicity.

"Well, both of you get your low-slung bodies out of here," demanded Puck. "My parents and my grandparents said we were lucky to live on land without any dogs and almost no people. And I think it should remain that way."

"This land is about to become a public park," I said. "Public means dogs are welcome. We're even coming to the opening party. Our owners are making us masks for the ball."

"What opening party?" demanded Puck.

"Don't you pay any attention to humans?" I asked him.

"Not like you dogs," sneered Puck. "I'm not a pet." He made it sound like a put-down. "I live in the biggest trees in the neighborhood. I can see over the treetops. The rest of you are lucky to get one tree to a yard. I got a good thing going on up here."

"Well, you're going to have to learn to share," I told him.

"Why should I?" he demanded.

"Tell him to park his big, bushy tail somewhere else," squeaked Jasper.

"One flick of my furry foot and flea you later," said Puck.

"I'd like to put his big mouth in a mask and muzzle it," said Felicity.

I couldn't have agreed with her more. Puck scampered away.

"Ah, there you are, children," said Mr. Fernbach when he saw everyone.

He turned to Miss Macintosh. "The press will love all those little children and pets in their masks dancing around and around." He rubbed his hands together at the very thought of it. "I'm glad so many of you have shown up, and brought your pets with you. Artists are here who will help you. You'll need to get your pets to sit still."

At the words *sit still*, Bernie bounded around the room. Buddy followed him, and so did Spencer, the little Chihuahua. It was chaos.

Fortunately, staying still was one of my particular skills. Jill and Gwen worked quietly with an artist named Jed. The frame for my wire mask was finished first.

"Ask him to make a mask for a flea!" begged Jasper.

"Gwen and Jill don't even know you exist," I reminded him.

"If I had a mask, they'd see me," said Jasper.

Jed helped Gwen and Jill put strips of newspaper

dunked in flour and water over the wire frame. Personally, I thought the flour mixture could have used a little salami.

I looked around for that nice Miss Macintosh who had been eating salami yesterday. She was in a corner eating again. She didn't seem very interested in the mask making. She smelled like baloney today. I like baloney too.

WIRE SCREEN FORM

TORN STRIPS OF NEWSPAPER

FLOUR AND WATER

HOW TO MAKE PAPIER-MÂCHÉ

Soon all the rough masks were done. The artist volunteers hung them on pegs to dry. It was very strange to see our faces hung on the wall. All of us were very silent.

"Tomorrow you'll come in and paint them," said Mr. Fernbach. "The more colorful the better!"

"I think Fletcher would look good in a little glitter," said Gwen.

"Great idea," said Jill. "We'll make him shine like the moon."

FLETCHER SHINING LIKE THE MOON

"Glitter," said Felicity, wagging her tail. "I just love glitter."

"You'd look good in glitter too," I told Felicity.

"Don't tell her that!" shrieked Jasper into my ear. "Glitter was Gwen and Jill's idea. She doesn't need glitter. You're the dog who does."

"It's a dance," I reminded Jasper. "There's no such thing as too much glitter at a dance."

"I thought you were the dog who hated dancing," said Jasper in a rather grumpy voice.

"Well, maybe I won't dance, but there's no reason

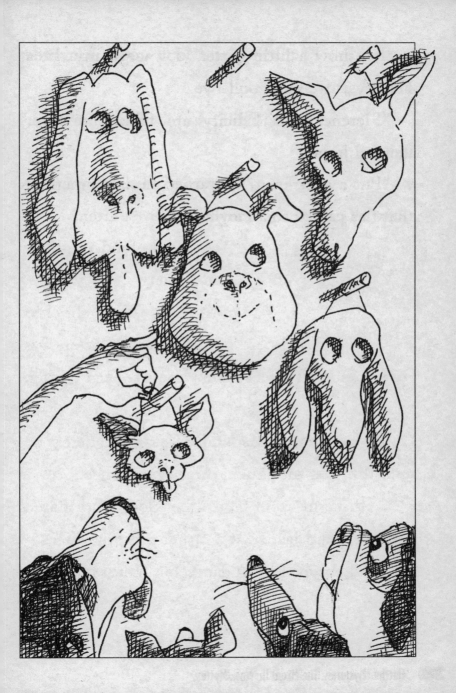

not to show a little glitter." I wagged my tail at Felicity as we said good-bye.

"Fletcher and Felicity are falling in love," taunted Jasper.

"Put a sock in it," I warned him. Sometimes that flea can be so annoying.

Four

Chew on That, You Rodent!

The next day Jill and Gwen couldn't wait till we got to the McKrieger house to check out our masks. Gwen carried some special glitter nail polish that she had gotten from her aunt Evie for her birthday.

"It's purple," she said. "Don't you think a deep purple moon will go well with Fletcher's brown-and-white spots?" asked Gwen.

"Purple with glitter! You'll outshine all those other dogs," shrieked Jasper. "You'll be the only long-eared pretty purple puppy at the party."

"Purple does go with my brown eyes," I admitted.

As we walked up to the house, I noticed something strange. I could hear the birds tweeting in the woods, but there was a sound missing.

I didn't hear Puck up there in the trees. I wondered where he was.

Then when we got into the house, I didn't wonder anymore.

The floor was covered with half-chewed little pieces of papier-mâché.

"Oh, no!" screamed Jill. "Our masks . . ."

I looked up. My mouth fell open, but that was nothing compared to the way my mask looked. Where my snout should have been there was a big hole.

I heard a low growl behind me. Roger was standing under his mask, except that his distinctive bulldog nose had been deformed into another gaping hole. There was little Felicity's dainty

distinctive pointed dachshund nose—destroyed by some dastardly villain.

All the kids were shrieking at once, but the dogs were just as upset. It was our faces that had been attacked.

Miss Macintosh was sweeping up the remains of the masks. I sniffed. While all the kids and dogs were losing their heads over losing our heads, I smelled salami.

I made my way over to Miss Macintosh. Her cell phone rang again. "I think the squirrels got in last night," I heard her say. Then she was silent. "I can't talk now. I'm at work."

Just then Mr. Fernbach arrived. "Oh, no!" he shouted. "What happened?"

"I don't know exactly," said Miss Macintosh. "When I got in this morning, all the masks had holes chewed through them. I'm pretty sure it was the squirrels. I doubt if we'll have time to make new masks for the pets before the dance. The kids' masks weren't touched."

"That's so sad," said Jill. "I really wanted Fletcher to be able to dance at the ball."

"Would squirrels have done this?" asked Gwen. "Why would they have chewed only the noses?"

"Who knows?" asked Jill.

"I can't believe your mask was ruined and we won't go to the ball," wailed Jasper, although secretly I was actually quite happy. Now Felicity wouldn't see how awkward my belly looked when I danced.

"Hold it! Hold it!" said Mr. Fernbach. "Are we going to let a few squirrelly invaders stop us? I've already alerted the media that there are going to be pets dancing in masks at the ball, and there will be."

"But the dance is tomorrow night! The masks are ruined!" said Miss Macintosh.

"I still think there's something funny about the fact that only the noses were attacked," said Gwen, tapping her braces, something she always did when she thought there was a mystery going on.

TAP-TAP-TAP-TAP-TAP

CLOSE-UP OF GWEN TAPPING HER BRACES

"What do you think?" asked Jill.

"Maybe someone wanted us to think the squirrels did it, but it was a *human* who went after the noses," said Gwen.

Miss Macintosh looked at her funny.

"Gwen's got a nose for mysteries," Jill explained.

"Does she ever!" said Jasper, hopping up and down and rubbing his antennae together. He likes mysteries as much as Gwen does, but the truth is he has the brainpower of a flea. He is always jumping to conclusions, and they're often wrong.

"Well," said Mr. Fernbach with a smile, "I don't think we want to call in the police for a nose job. It could be bad publicity. Meanwhile, I've got reporters coming to the dance. I promised them pets in masks."

"We can make them again," said Isabella. "It's a sunny day and we can dry them outside in the sun."

"We could bring in blow-dryers," interrupted Jill. "That would help the masks dry more quickly."

"That's the kind of can-do spirit I like," said Mr. Fernbach.

Felicity bounded up to me. She said, "Imagine the gall of that rodent, chewing our noses off. I'd like to get my teeth into his nose."

"Gwen thinks there might be a human hand behind it," said Jasper. "Let's help her solve the mystery. Fletcher is very good at that!"

"Actually, I'm very good at taking a nap," I said.

Felicity looked a little disappointed.

Fiedler Fernbach and the artists helped the kids patch up the masks. Then they took them out in the sun to dry.

Gwen and Jill and some other kids ran home and borrowed their mothers' hair dryers. Jill told me to stay with Miss Macintosh to guard the masks.

Miss Macintosh sat down under a tree and unwrapped another salami sandwich. I think it was Hungarian salami. I have to say that she had terrific taste in food.

She didn't seem very interested in me, and less interested in the masks lying in the sun.

"You'd think a ranger would patrol," complained Jasper.

"I don't think she's that kind of ranger," I explained to him. "Besides, rangers have to eat, too."

"So let's help Gwen solve the mystery," said

Jasper. "You *know* it will impress Felicity."

"If she doesn't like me for myself, there's nothing I can do," I said with a yawn. I had other things on my mind besides solving mysteries or even Felicity. Miss Macintosh took out a piece of salami and gently handed it to me. I wagged my tail at her. She looked worried. I wondered if it had anything to do with the cell phones calls she kept getting. Whoever called her did seem to annoy her. Finally she took out her cell phone. "Aunt Julie, we've got to talk. . . . You . . ."

Before she could finish the sentence, Gwen, Jill, and Isabella came running through the woods carrying their hair dryers.

"Aunt Julie . . . it *is* cute. You can't stop cute. . . ." She listened and made a face.

"No!" she said. She hung up the phone quickly as Mr. Fernbach came around the corner.

HUNGARIAN SALAMI

Mr. Fernbach brought out extension cords and the kids got busy drying their masks. It got to be pretty noisy with all those hair dryers going at once. I was sure glad for my long silky ears, which covered up at least some of the noise. Miss Macintosh got up, giving me another little scrap of her salami.

"She's my favorite ranger," I said to Jasper.

"She's the only ranger you know," Jasper reminded me. "Now will you get to work and investigate who ruined the masks?"

Above the roar of the hair dryers, I heard a chattering noise.

I looked up. Puck's tail was wrapped around a low-hanging branch. His little front paws were covering his ears.

"What's that noise! It's scaring the birds!"

"There you are, you scoundrel squirrel!" shouted

NOAH

Jasper. "Our humans are too smart for you. They're fixing up their masks. Chew on that, you rodent!"

"What's going on?" demanded Puck.

"We spoiled your little plan to spoil our fun," said Felicity. "The masked ball will go on."

"What little plan?" Puck asked.

"Don't tell me you didn't take a bite out of every nose," growled Roger. "Even mine. And a bulldog has a noble nose."

Puck looked down at me. "Hey, Lard-gut, how come you're so quiet all of a sudden?"

"Sometimes it pays to listen," I said.

"Well, somebody shut those noisemakers off!" demanded Puck. "This is a forest, for goodness' sake, not a beauty parlor."

"Fletcher," Felicity whispered, "say something to that nasty squirrel."

"Yeah," muttered Jasper. "She thinks you're afraid

of a rodent. Show a little teeth."

I would have, but I had a little piece of salami stuck in my teeth.

A LITTLE PIECE OF
SALAMI STUCK
IN FLETCHER'S TEETH

Five

Liar! Liar!
Pants Really Are
on Fire!

Maybe it was the salami, maybe it was the droning sound of the hair dryers, maybe it was using my brain cells to try to figure out what was going on, but I fell asleep in the afternoon sun. As I closed my eyes, I noticed that Felicity, Roger, Spencer, and all the other dogs were also taking a little snooze. We dogs know what to do with a summer afternoon.

My nap didn't last long.

"Wake up! Wake up!" shouted Jumping Jasper. "There's a mystery to be solved."

"Look, you hyper-flapping flea, leave me alone.

The masks are fixed. Who cares whether it was a rodent or a human? In the long run, it really doesn't make a difference."

"No, no, it's not that," said Jasper. "Don't you smell something?"

I sniffed the air, hoping for a whiff of Miss Macintosh eating some salami. Instead I smelled the faint odor of smoke.

The wind was swirling in different directions. At first I couldn't figure out where the smoke was coming from.

Naturally, Jasper couldn't be patient. He kept bouncing on my nose. "Find it! Find it!" he kept at me.

"I will if you get off my nose. I use it for smelling, you know. Just back off! Be quiet and let me concentrate."

"You're taking an awfully long time to investigate,"

complained Jasper. "Let's run around and see if we can find the fire."

"It's a waste of time to run in circles," I warned him. "Just be quiet and let me listen and smell!"

I lifted my nose into the air. The humans had finished drying their masks, and they were now applying feathers, glitter, and paint to their master- pieces on picnic tables. When humans are really into creating something they kind of go into a trance. Some of them even forget to eat. None of them seemed to smell the smoke. But I have a much better nose than any human, so it really wasn't surprising.

I took a deep sniff. I definitely

FLETCHER'S NOSE
SNIFFING smelled something bitter and harsh, nothing at all like a barbecue. It seemed to be coming from the front porch where I had first

met Miss Macintosh eating a salami sandwich.

I climbed up the steps to the porch. All the adults were down on the lawn working with the kids at the picnic tables. The porch was empty. But the smell was definitely stronger up on the porch.

The rocking chair in the corner was swinging back and forth. I looked up. There was nobody in it.

I sniffed around the rocker. The smell was definitely stronger here. I followed it. Then I saw it. There was an outlet right near the rocker with extension cords that had been used to plug in the hair dryers. The plastic coating on the wire had been chewed or cut through. Little sparks flew in all directions!

I barked to warn the humans that something had to be done.

"Fletcher, be quiet!" yelled Jill. "We're working."

"He's probably looking for food," said Isabella. "Your dog is always hungry."

I ran to the edge of the porch and barked again.

"He probably found a piece of salami," said Gwen.

Humans can be so dense sometimes. They keep us around as watchdogs. Then when we actually watch something that needs their attention, they ignore us.

One of the sparks from the frayed wires flew into a corner where there was a pile of leaves. The leaves began to smolder.

I had to do something. I ran down the steps and threw myself on Miss Macintosh, tugging at her hand. She had a paintbrush with purple paint on it, and I got a wide purple streak just under Florida.

"Fletcher!" she cried. "What are you doing?"

I gently kept her hand in my teeth, careful not to press down. Dogs' teeth are very sharp, even on a gentle dog like me. But I had to get her to come with me.

"He wants you to go with him!" said Gwen with a tap to her braces. I could have kissed the girl.

"I told you she was brilliant!" said Jasper.

Gwen and Jill followed Miss Macintosh and me up the porch where Felicity and Roger were jumping up and down.

"Fire!" yelled Miss Macintosh. "Kids—get off the porch! Mr. Fernbach! Fire!"

Mr. Fernbach came running up to the porch. He tried to stamp the fire out with his feet. One of the sparks landed on his pants and his pants began to smolder. He didn't seem to notice.

Gosh, these humans needed help. I ran back on the porch.

"Fletcher, no!" screamed Jill.

But I had to. I ran up and sunk my teeth into

Mr. Fernbach's pants legs. He tried to shake me off. "Go away, dog!" he yelled. Then he looked down and noticed that his pant leg was on fire.

He swatted it. Miss Macintosh came out of the back of the house, carrying a fire extinguisher. Mr. Fernbach grabbed it from her, and aimed the nozzle first at his pant leg and then at the fire in the corner. Very quickly the fire fizzled.

Mr. Fernbach knelt down. "Those darned squirrels. They must have chewed through the wires. It could have been a disaster."

"It was Fletcher who saved the day!" said Jill proudly. "He was barking up here, and we all ignored him, but he came and got Miss Macintosh."

Mr. Fernbach looked at me. "To think that I thought you were a lazy hound. Why, you saved the house and maybe the whole park! What's that dog's name again?"

"Fletcher," said Jill. "He's shaped like the earth. I painted a purple glitter moon on his mask."

"Well, I'm going to make sure that he gets a special mention at the dance tomorrow," said Mr. Fernbach. "Now, boys and girls, I want you to get your masks. We'll put them in plastic bags in the storeroom so the squirrels don't get them. Miss Macintosh will give you tags to put on the bags."

Miss Macintosh put down her salami sandwich and wiped her hands on her jeans. Her hands smelled of salami.

"You're a hero," Felicity told me.

I felt myself blushing.

She batted her eyes at me. Dachshunds have particularly attractive eyes. "Be sure to save a dance for me," she whispered.

"He doesn't dance," said Jasper.

"Oh," said Felicity.

"It's just that I look so silly," I said.

"You have a fine figure for dancing," said Felicity. "Maybe tomorrow you'll feel like it."

"Don't count on it," said Jasper.

"Maybe I will," I said.

"Your belly will wiggle. Your ears will jiggle," warned Jasper into my ear.

I sighed. "Jasper's right," I said to Felicity. "I'm just not a dancer."

She looked as disappointed as Jill had, but really, what could I do?

Six

Who Would Ruin the Dance?

In late afternoon on the night of the ball, the sky turned dark and gloomy. Gray clouds hung down lower than my belly.

"Oh, no!" said Jill, when she looked out the window. "It looks awful. Do you think they're going to call off the ball?"

"Curse this foul weather," said Jasper.

"A rainy evening in summer can be very nice," I reminded him. "There's nothing wrong with snuggling in a corner chewing a book."

"Not on tonight of all nights!" said Jasper.

"You'll miss Felicity in her cute little mask."

I thought about it. Nap . . . Felicity . . . nap . . . Felicity. It was a hard choice.

"I called the McKrieger Park hot line," said Jill's mother. "The weather report says the thunder showers should be brief. If necessary, they'll have the dance in the house. We'll go as soon as Gwen gets here."

Gwen arrived a little while later.

"You're late!" insisted Jill.

"I know," said Gwen. "But I've got a good excuse. I looked up McKrieger Park on the computer. The name of the cousin who tried to stop the park is Macintosh."

"The ranger, Miss Macintosh?" asked Jill.

"Who else could it be?" said Gwen. "I bet she's secretly been plotting to ruin the dance from the beginning."

"Isn't Gwen brilliant," gushed Jasper. "If you had used your brain cells instead of your salami cells, you could have solved the mystery too."

I frowned. I found it hard to believe that Miss Macintosh was behind the things that had happened at the park.

"You're just disappointed that the culprit turned out to be someone who likes salami," said Jasper, reading my mind. "Well, you'll have to learn that not all salami-lovers are good people."

I sighed. Maybe Jasper was right, but somehow I just couldn't believe that the same Miss Macintosh who had fed me salami could have smashed all our masks and tried to set the park on fire. It made me sad.

When we arrived in the park at dusk, the woods looked even darker and spookier than ever. I heard a noise above me.

"I thought humans don't go outside in the rain," complained Puck.

"They have umbrellas," I explained.

Puck shook his little fist. He flung down a nut at me.

"Cut that out!" I yelled.

"Come on, Fletcher," said Jill, pulling on my leash. "Why are you making those silly noises at that squirrel?"

"Humans," sniffed Puck. "Your owner pulls your leash and you go with her."

My mood got as dark as the weather. I was certainly in no mood for a dance.

Up at the house, Mr. Fernbach was all atwitter. Sasha Hughes, star of the local television show *Sasha Says*, had arrived dressed in a cute little feathered mask that made her look like a peacock. Mr. Fernbach had on a matching peacock mask. Those

peacock feathers were going to look pretty sad in a downpour. The public was starting to arrive. A woman came in wearing a squirrel mask with a big squirrel tail on her head. I wondered if Puck had seen her, and if it bothered him to see his head on a human.

"Okay, children," said Mr. Fernbach. "Come inside and get your masks. Move quickly. The dance is about to start, and the cameramen want to get the opening parade. Remember, your masks are in the storeroom in the plastic bags with your names on them."

Gwen and Jill ran inside to get their bags.

"Hey!" shouted Gwen. "All our names are gone!"

Each and every tag had disappeared.

"I must have left the door to the storeroom open, and those darned squirrels came in and took the tags," said Miss Macintosh.

Gwen began to tap her braces. "I don't think squirrels would do that!" she said.

"Why not?" asked Miss Macintosh. "They ate through your masks, and started a fire, and now they went after your name tags."

"Maybe," said Gwen. "Or maybe you want everyone to think that's what happened." She gave Miss Macintosh a meaningful glance.

Mr. Fernbach clapped his hands. "Everybody. We don't have time to deal with this little setback. We'll just open the bags and you'll find the right masks. . . ."

Suddenly the lights in the house went out. It was as black as my nose inside the storeroom.

"Don't panic, everybody!" shouted Mr. Fernbach. "Just grab any bag and put on a mask. We have to get outside right away. The TV cameras want to broadcast this live. Just get out there. . . ."

A thunderclap drowned out whatever he was saying next.

I felt something shiver beside me. It was Felicity. "I hate thunder," she said.

"Me too," I said. "It reminds me of times I lived on the streets."

"You lived on the streets?" she said. She sounded shocked. I was a little embarrassed. Maybe I shouldn't have told her.

Jill leaned down and put a mask on my face. It didn't feel quite right. In the darkness, somebody reached down and put a mask on my rear end. Apparently it landed right on top of Jasper.

Spencer, the little Chihuahua, ran under my legs.

"I don't want to wear my mask," he said. "It pinches."

"Hey," said Jasper. "I think your mask landed on Fletcher's tail."

"Leave it there, please," said Spencer.

"It's actually kind of cozy," said Jasper.

Just then Sasha Hughes came running in. "We're ready to go live. Somebody pulled the fuse box for the house, but luckily our cameras and lights work on generators."

"So it wasn't the thunder," said Gwen. She began to tap her braces. Or at least she tried to tap them through the pink and green feathers she had on her mask.

"Let's go, people and pets!" shouted Mr. Fernbach. "Just follow my voice and come outside." He opened the door to the house. We were greeted by a huge uproar of laughter. I could hear the sound of TV cameras whirring.

"Oh, this is adorable!" cooed Sasha Hughes. "Look at that dachshund with the face of a basset hound."

"And that basset hound has two heads!" shouted another voice.

"One's a bulldog and one's a Chihuahua! Is that not the cleverest thing you ever saw?" gushed Sasha Hughes. "Fiedler Fernbach, you're brilliant! Quick! Get a picture!"

"What's going on?" demanded Jasper. "I can't see a thing."

Through the slits in my mask, I could see Felicity wearing my head. Roger was wearing the head of a Lhasa apso. I must have had on the head of a bulldog. We all did look pretty silly.

But there was one adult who wasn't laughing. Miss Macintosh was standing to the side, talking into her cell phone.

"Come on, everybody! The dance is about to begin!" shouted Mr. Fernbach.

"Not yet!" shouted Gwen. " I know who ruined

our masks. I know who started the fire. I know who removed the name tags. I know who pulled the fuses on the house."

"Gwen solved it all without you!" muttered the flea on my rear.

"Maybe," I admitted. But Gwen had forgotten one thing. When the fuses were pulled Miss Macintosh had been with us. I had smelled her. It had to be something else. But who could have tried to ruin the dance? I needed to find out and I needed to find out fast.

Seven

Trip the Light Fantastic

Gwen and Jill slunk quietly over to where Miss Macintosh was on her cell phone. Miss Macintosh was so intent on her phone call, she didn't notice us. Adults tend to ignore anything either under four feet or with four feet.

"Aunt Julie, where are you?" demanded Miss Macintosh. "I know you're here. . . ."

"You!" shouted Gwen, before Miss Macintosh could finish. "You tried to ruin this dance from the beginning."

Mr. Fernbach rushed over.

"What's going on?" he demanded.

"The name of the person who sued about the park was Macintosh," said Gwen. "Miss Macintosh has been trying to make sure that this celebration was ruined."

Miss Macintosh slapped her phone shut. "It's true that my aunt wanted to ruin the celebration," she said. "She thought the park should belong to her, and she wanted to live here alone. I'm trying to find her."

"You tried to help her," said Gwen, interrupting her. "You ruined our masks. You cut the wires. You threw away our name tags—all so your aunt could drive people out of the park."

"No, I didn't," protested Miss Macintosh. "I told my aunt that the land belonged to the people."

"I didn't know that humans had pet ants that they cared so much about," whispered Jasper. I

could tell he was excited. If an ant could be that important, maybe Gwen would notice a flea.

PET ANT

"It's not that kind of an ant," I explained. "It's a human relative."

"Why can't humans just have one word for what they mean?"

Up above me, I heard a cackling sound. Puck was up there, holding the sides of his belly.

"Dumb humans!" he said. "Look at them blaming each other. This party will never come off."

"You . . . you chewed on the wires. . . . You pulled the fuses and ate our noses!" Jasper shouted up at him. "You wanted the humans to be blamed."

Puck chuckled.

"Fletcher, do something!" shouted Jasper. "That squirrel is getting away with it."

I wrinkled my brow. I looked up at Puck. Could he have done it all? I doubted it. Then under a tree, I saw the shadow of a giant squirrel. Was it one of Puck's relatives? No, it was that human I had seen coming to the party in a squirrel mask. Then I remembered. Miss Macintosh had thanked her aunt for the salami sandwich. There was more than one human in the park that night who loved salami, and one of them was a salami-eating snake in the grass. Or squirrel in the grass. And not even a real squirrel at that.

The person in the squirrel mask had a giant pair of wirecutters, and she was about to cut the wires from the TV generator.

I pounced.

The squirrel's head came rolling off. I fell back in shock. I'm strong, but I didn't think I was strong enough to knock a squirrel's head off. But I knew it wasn't a squirrel.

"Aunt Julie!" shouted Miss Macintosh. "I knew you were here. What are you doing now?"

"One way or another, you're not going to televise a party to celebrate what should have been mine!" shouted Aunt Julie Macintosh.

"Who is she?" demanded Puck. "And why did she come to the park dressed like a giant me?"

"She's not a squirrel. She's the one who tried to ruin the dance," I said.

"Mr. Fernbach, meet my aunt," said Miss Macintosh. "I've been worried about her. She was furious that there was going to be a party. I tried to persuade her to be a graceful loser, but she would do anything to spoil the party. Aunt Julie! How could you have tried to set fire to the place? The park was Old Man McKrieger's dream."

"I wasn't going to set the place on fire," argued the lady. "I was just going to cut the wires so the cameras wouldn't work. I tried to pull the fuses, but all that did was turn off the lights in the house."

"You were cutting the wires just like you did on the hair dryers!" insisted Miss Macintosh. "You almost set the whole place on fire yesterday."

"What hair dryers!" demanded Aunt Julie. "I confess I snuck in one day and smashed all those cute noses. I hate cute. I just knew all those cute masks would make everybody love the park. Then you just made cuter masks. And I didn't have time to destroy them. I tried to stop the dance from being televised, but I never cut any wires—until today. I just couldn't stand the idea that everybody was going to dance on land that should have belonged to me. And on top of that it was going to be cute."

I heard a chuckle up above me.

"Puck!" I exclaimed. "It was you who chewed on the wires that day, wasn't it? *You* chewed on the wires for the hair dryers, not Miss Macintosh's aunt."

"I didn't know it would start a fire," admitted Puck. "The noise was killing me."

"Why did your aunt take the name tags?" asked Mr. Fernbach.

"Yes, Aunt Julie!" demanded Miss Macintosh. "Why did you take the name tags and cause the mix-up?"

Puck was holding his stomach, he was laughing so hard. That's when I realized. There were two culprits. And they both had squirrel heads. Miss Macintosh's aunt hadn't taken the name tags. It was just the kind of prank that puckish Puck prized.

"Those little pieces of paper smelled so good," snickered Puck.

"They smelled of salami, you little rodent," I told him. "You caused the great mask mix-up."

"And I'm glad," said Puck.

"Where did you hide them?" I growled at him.

Puck just laughed. "Where you'll never find them," he taunted.

But Puck didn't know my sniffer. Those name tags still had just the slightest scent of salami on them because that's what Miss Macintosh had been eating. I dug into the soft leaves. All the name tags were buried under the leaves, with little squirrel bites taken out of them.

Gwen watched me, tapping her braces.

"Our name tags," said Jill.

"And look," said Gwen. "There are little squirrel footprints in the mud leading from the house."

I nodded my big head up and down.

"Mr. Fernbach," yelled Gwen. "Come over here! Maybe Miss Macintosh's aunt didn't take our name tags."

Mr. Fernbach came over with Miss Macintosh and her aunt.

"Hmm," he said. "It does look like this was the work of squirrels."

"I told you I didn't take the name tags, but now that I see how silly all these pets look in their mixed-up masks, I wish I had thought of it," said Aunt Julie Macintosh.

"Aunt Julie, don't you realize that this land belongs to everyone now? You lost the lawsuit. You even wore a mask to the party. Can't you see this is now a park for everyone to enjoy."

Aunt Julie sniffed. "No!"

"Then I think you should go home," said Miss Macintosh, taking her arm. "As a ranger for the park, I forbid you to come here again. You've done too much mischief."

"I don't *want* to set foot on this park again," said Aunt Julie.

"Go home and watch it on TV," said Mr. Fernbach. "Kids, we've got a party to put on. Everybody, let's keep this little nutty incident to ourselves—not a word of this to the reporters."

Puck clunked him on the head with a pine nut.

"Stop being a mischief-maker, too," I warned Puck. "Share the park, or get out."

"Oh yeah, who's going to make me?" asked Puck.

I looked around at all my four-footed friends. "We can chase squirrels until the cows come home," I told him. "You'll get really, really tired."

"You said you weren't the squirrel-chasing kind of dog," he said.

"My friends are," I said.

Puck looked worried.

Felicity wagged her tail. I couldn't see her face through the mask, but I knew she was smiling.

"Everybody," shouted Mr. Fernbach. "We've got a midsummer fling to put on!"

The musicians were dressed in high socks with bells on them. The recorder players and fiddlers began to play a merry tune.

"Come on, Fletcher!" shouted Jill. She dragged me into a circle right next to Isabella and Felicity. Felicity was dancing prettily on her back feet. Her head was that of a basset hound painted to look like a purple glittering moon.

I couldn't help myself—something in the rhythm of the music made my paws start to stomp. I lifted myself onto my back paws, and I was dancing.

"Whoops!" shouted Jasper from my rear end.

"Fletcher is a two-headed dancer," shouted

Gwen. "Spencer's mask landed on his behind. I'm going to dance with Fletcher's tail."

Gwen didn't know it, but she was dancing with one very, very happy flea.

Over to the side, I saw Jill's mother holding out a cashew to Puck. He took it daintily and then fled up a tree. Then he did a one-hundred-eighty-degree turn and held on to the tree upside down. He nibbled his cashew.

After the dance was over, Jasper and I went and rested under the tree. Miss Macintosh came over to me. She looked down at my mask.

"Thank you," she whispered. I didn't know how she knew, but she knew that I knew she was innocent from the beginning. Then she put a little salami through the hole in my mask. I chewed. It was Italian salami.

Up above me, Puck was chewing his cashew.

"This is one tasty nut," he said. "I haven't tasted anything quite like it."

"A lot of cashews come from Brazil," I said. "One of the many good thing about living around humans is that they like food from around the world." I showed him where Brazil was on the map on my body.

"Maybe it won't be so bad having them in the park," said Puck.

"If you stop doing things to drive them away, they'll bring treats from all over the world to taste. Wait till you taste French fries," Felicity told him.

"You know, Fletcher," said Puck. "Maybe you're right. I guess I could even get used to sharing my park with you."

"What about me?" squeaked a voice from my rear end.

"You look mighty silly in that Chihuahua mask," said Puck.

"Never mind," said Jasper. "Gwen and I actually got to dance."

Mr. Fernbach went to the microphone. "Ladies and gentlemen, boys and girls. This is indeed a special day. Many people worked hard. But we have a special thanks to one of the hounds who saved the day. I'd like Jill and her dog, Fletcher, to come lead the next dance. Let's cheer them as they trip the light fantastic."

"What's that?" asked Puck.

"I think it means to dance," I said. "You just let the music sink down into your paws. Then your hips begin to sway."

Puck's tail began to twitch back and forth in time with the beat.

"That's it," I said.

Jill held out her hands to me. Felicity's tail was wagging to the music. I got up and I put my paws in Jill's hands. We led the dance.